Some Dog!

Mary Casanova

Pictures by Ard Hoyt

SCHOLASTIC INC.
New York   Toronto   London   Auckland   Sydney
Mexico City   New Delhi   Hong Kong   Buenos Aires

For Eric, who is some son
—M.C.

To William Calhoun,
who rescued me
—A.H.

ISBN-13: 978-0-545-14258-8
ISBN-10: 0-545-14258-X

Text copyright © 2007 by Mary Casanova.
Illustrations copyright © 2007 by Ard Hoyt.
All rights reserved. Published by Scholastic Inc.,
557 Broadway, New York, NY 10012, by arrangement with
Farrar, Straus and Giroux, Inc. SCHOLASTIC and associated logos
are trademarks and/or registered trademarks of Scholastic Inc.

9 10 11 12 13 14/0

08

12 11 10 9 8 7 6 5 4 3 2 1

Printed in the U.S.A.

First Scholastic printing, January 2009

Designed by Robbin Gourley and Symon Chow

George had a good life.

When the woman read the
newspaper, George had a place to rest
his weary head.

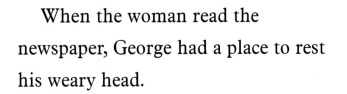

When the man chopped
wood, George studied a
thousand scents on the wind.

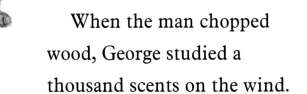

And when they went fishing,
George, who couldn't swim, rode
in the middle, steady and still.

"You're some dog," said the woman.

"Some dog!" said the man.

But the day another dog arrived, everything changed.

"He must be a stray," said the woman.

"Looks like he's here to stay," said the man.

"*Wa-roooo!*" cried George. "*Wa-roo-roo-roo-roo!*"

"Ya-yippity, yappity,

Like a jackrabbit, the stray leaped back and forth.

"*Ya-yippity, yappity, yeep-yeep-yeep!*"

Then he zipped around the room three times.

yeep-yeep-yeep!"

"What a lively dog!" said the woman.
"Let's call him Zippity," said the man.

Now, when the newspaper arrived, Zippity snatched it, flew over the couch, and dropped it at the woman's feet.

"Good dog!"

When the man chopped wood, Zippity backflipped and caught sticks in midair.

"Amazing!"

When the man and the woman biked to the corner store, Zippity ran ahead with the grocery list. By the time they arrived, the shop owner had the groceries packed up and ready to go.

"What a dog!"

And when they all went fishing, Zippity jumped from George's back, from lap to lap until . . . he dove, caught a fish, and swam to shore.

"That Zippity is *some dog*!"

That night at dinner, George was too tired to beg for food.

At bedtime, he was exhausted.
But Zippity snored—

zeep,

zeep,

zeep

—in his sleep.

One day, George smelled rain on the wind. Before long, thunder grumbled. It boom-boom-clanged and rumbled. George didn't mind.

But with each clap of thunder, Zippity raced in crazy circles. He plinked . . . He chewed . . . He dashed . . . and crashed until finally . . .

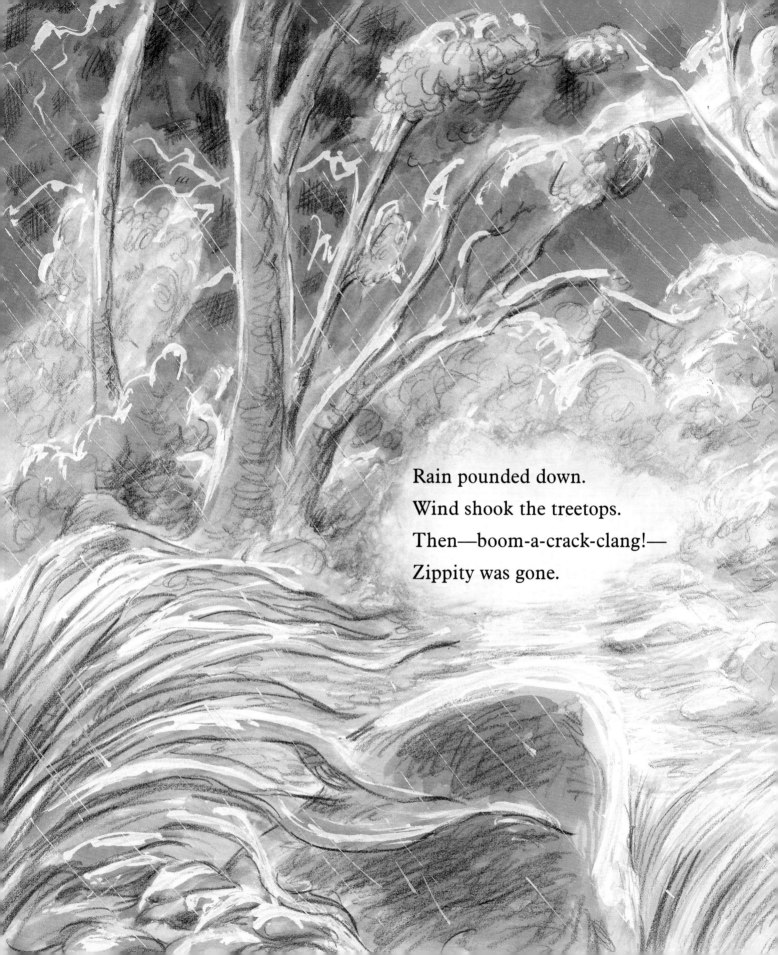

Rain pounded down.
Wind shook the treetops.
Then—boom-a-crack-clang!—
Zippity was gone.

"He'll get lost!"

"It's a terrible storm!"

But George thumped his tail.
At last, he'd have his bed all to
himself.

"George," begged the woman, "go find Zippity."
George stretched and groaned.
"C'mon, George," the man pleaded.
"Here, George," the woman said. "Smell this."

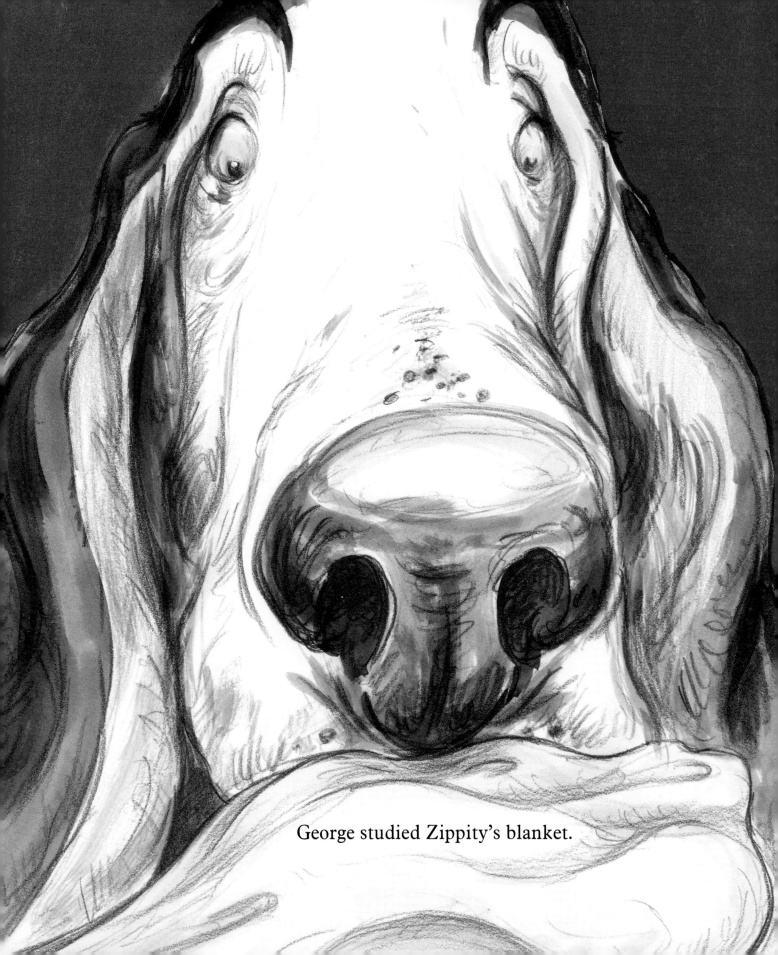

George studied Zippity's blanket.

If there was one thing George could do, it was follow a smell.

Through whipping wind and needle rain, George led the way. Nose to the ground, he sniffed and whiffed, snorted and twitched.

He smelled a thousand scents, but followed only one.

Past a farmhouse in shambles, a clothesline, and thorny brambles, George tracked the scent. When the man and woman turned back, George pressed on, following his nose.

Up steep steps and down he went.
To the top of a seesaw . . .

to the ground again.

Along a slippery rail, over a rotted pine, down along the valley through the swampy, murky mire: George kept going, until his nose led him to a shivery, shaking, wet and quaking . . .

Zippity!

Stuck.

In the thick, oozy muck.

"*Wa-roo-*

Zippity whimpered. Zippity whined. He twisted and turned, he wriggled and churned. But the harder he tried to reach the bank, the deeper . . . and deeper . . . and deeper he sank!

"*Wa-roooo!*" George cried.

roo-roo-roo!"

Then George stretched himself across a log. He grabbed Zippity's collar and held fast. Slow and steady, steady and slow—George tugged and pulled, pulled and tugged until . . .

Out Zippity POPPED!

The dogs touched noses. Then George led the way.

He sniffed and whiffed, snorted and twitched, following the trail, through the swampy, murky mire, over a rotted pine . . .

down a slippery slide . . .

until . . .

"It's Zippity!" they cried.

"You found him!"

"Oh, George! You're some dog!" said the man.

"*Our* dog," said the woman.

From that day on, George and Zippity got along just fine.
George always had a place to rest his weary head.

Every day, he studied a thousand scents on the wind.

And when they all went fishing, George rode in the middle, steady and still.

And most nights, George didn't mind sharing—

zeep,

zeep,

zeep

—even in his sleep.